To my Popie, for teaching me how to draw a star all those years ago.
And to my boys, Ben and Jack, for inspiring the song that became the story.
Have another milkshake for the road. . . .
K. N.

To my granddaughter, Nana, who always cheers me up with
her adorable smile, and to my husband, Ko, for all his support.
This book is for them with deepest gratitude.
C. O.

CANDLEWICK PRESS

Text copyright © 2019 by Karl Newson • Illustrations copyright © 2019 by Chiaki Okada • Published by arrangement with Paper Crane Agency • All rights reserved. No part of this book may be reproduced, transmitted, or stored in an information retrieval system in any form or by any means, graphic, electronic, or mechanical, including photocopying, taping, and recording, without prior written permission from the publisher. • First U.S. edition 2019 • Library of Congress Catalog Card Number 2018961618 • ISBN 978-1-5362-0542-8 • This book was typeset in Alice. The illustrations were done in pencil. • Candlewick Press, 99 Dover Street, Somerville, Massachusetts 02144 • visit us at www.candlewick.com

Printed in Humen, Dongguan, China • 19 20 21 22 23 24 APS 10 9 8 7 6 5 4 3 2 1

For All the Stars Across the Sky

Karl Newson   illustrated by **Chiaki Okada**

At the end of the day,
when the sun is fading
and Luna is yawning . . .

it's time for pajamas,
teeth brushing,
and climbing into bed.

"Now close your eyes," says Mama,
"and we'll make a wish. . . .

For all the stars across the sky,
Big and little and bright,
Here's a wish from me to you
Before we say good night."

"I wish," says Luna,
"that we could fly like birds!"

"So let's be birds!" says Mama.
"Let's fly by mountaintops
and over patchwork fields,
just you, the clouds, and me."

"All the way around the world," says Luna,
"and over the deep blue sea...."

"Now I wish we could swim like fish!"

"Let's dip and dive," says Mama,
"among corals in every color,
just you, the whale song, and me."

"Oh, wow!" says Luna. "I feel so small...."

"Now I wish we were even smaller —
like ladybugs!"

"Let's catch a ride," says Mama,
"exploring the vines
and the twigs in the mud,
just you, the crickets, and me."

"Let's creep and climb!" says Luna.
"To the top of a dandelion that's as high
as the sky. . . . Oh, I know!
Should we be big again?"

"I wish we were big, really big—
like giants!"

"Let's gaze over treetops," says Mama,
"and stomp loudly down the lane,
just you, the birds, and me...."

"Let's *stomp, stomp, stomp* all the way
home to our giants' house,
because even giants sleep sometimes."

"And our giants' bed is just the right size,"
says Luna. "Just the right size
for you and me."

At the end of the day,
when the sun is fading
and Luna's eyes are closing,
it's time for turning out the lights,
snuggling into bed,
and dreaming sweet dreams....

"For all the stars across the sky,
Big and little and bright,
Here's a kiss from me to you
As we say good night."